ZONE 13

Time For...

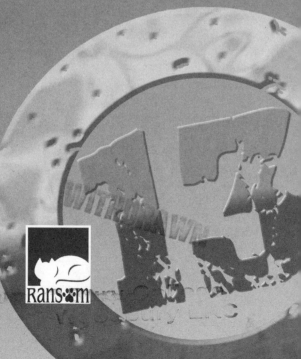

DAVID ORME

Rans✺m

Time Forest
by David Orme
Illustrated by Jorge Mongiovi and Ulises Carpintero
Cover photograph: © JovanCormac and Ekaterina Shvaygert

Published by Ransom Publishing Ltd.
Radley House, 8 St. Cross Road, Winchester, Hampshire, SO23 9HX, UK
www.ransom.co.uk

ISBN   978 184167 465 0

First published in 2011

Copyright © 2011 Ransom Publishing Ltd.

Illustrations copyright © 2011 Jorge Mongiovi and Ulises Carpintero

Printed in India by Imprint Digital Ltd.
Originally published in 1998 by Stanley Thornes Publishers Ltd.

A CIP catalogue record of this book is available from the British Library.

CONTENTS

NOT FOR THE PUBLIC TO KNOW
TOP SECRET
ZONE 13 FILES ONLY

4

LOST!

'It's your fault we're lost!'

The two girls glared at each other. All around them were trees. They had planned a morning's walk in the forest. Now they couldn't find their way back.

Sophie looked at the map again, but that made Chris even more cross.

Sophie didn't say anything. Chris had a terrible temper, but her rages didn't last long. She never sulked.

They started off again. This part of the forest had pine trees. The ground was covered in pine needles. Clumps of bracken grew here and there.

'Here's a path!'

'Which way shall we go?' asked Chris.

Sophie looked at her compass.

'It goes north to south. We need to go south.'

The path twisted and turned. Sophie looked at the compass again.

'I don't believe it! We're going west now!'

Just then, they heard the sound of someone talking in the distance.

'Great! There's someone coming!'

Sophie was worried.

'There's more than one person. They might be dangerous.'

'Let's hide and look at them. We can come out if they look O.K.'

They scrambled into the bracken at the side of the path.

Through the bracken, they saw two people in uniform.

They were both carrying guns.

NOT FOR THE PUBLIC TO KNOW

TOP SECRET

ZONE 13 FILES ONLY

2

DANGER OR DEATH

The girls decided not to show themselves. They didn't want to deal with soldiers carrying guns! They decided to wait five minutes, then follow them. The soldiers must be going somewhere.

After a while the path divided into two.

'That's typical!' said Chris. 'Now which way do we go?'

They chose the left-hand path. The forest got thicker and darker. Earlier, they had seen

and heard birds and squirrels. Now the forest was silent. It wasn't cold, but both girls shivered.

'I bet we've gone the wrong way again,' said Chris.

The path started to slope down. Below them, they could hear the sound of water.

Soon they reached a stream. It splashed down a small waterfall.

On the other side of the stream there was a tall fence. Razor wire ran along the top. The path crossed the stream on stepping stones, then ran along the side of the fence.

The girls crossed the stream. At that point there was a notice on the fence:

DANGER OF DEATH
KEEP OUT

CAPTURED

'How friendly!' said Chris.

Sophie looked at the razor wire.

'I don't think we'll try getting over it!' she said. 'There must be a gate, though. If we follow the path, we'll get to it. We might find a road there that will get us out of here.'

They looked through the fence. There was very little to see. The trees grew closely together.

The stream ran along by the path for a little way. The girls came to a place where the

water came gushing out of a big pipe. The pipe went under the path. They guessed that the stream came from inside the fence.

They were both very tired and thirsty. They were worried that they might still be lost when it got dark.

Chris took her camera out of her backpack. 'Go and stand over by that death notice. I'll take your photo,' she said. 'Smile!'

Suddenly, someone grabbed her from behind. 'Oh no you don't!'

Two soldiers were standing there. One of them held Chris's arm behind her back.

The other one was pointing a gun.

THE THIN MAN

'Who told you to come here and take photographs?'

The girls had been marched along the path until they reached a gate. Just inside the gate was a wooden building. They were now in a small office. A thin man in a plain suit was sitting behind a desk.

'No one did. We just got lost in the woods.'

The thin man picked up a telephone.

'Send Smith in here.'

He put the phone down.

'Stand over there. Against that wall.'

A soldier came in, carrying a box. The thin man opened the box and took a camera out of it. He photographed each girl in turn.

'Get those pictures checked out. And lock up these two. I'll have more questions for them later.'

The girls were pushed into an empty room and the door was locked.

Chris was really angry.

'They can't do this to us!'

She banged on the door.

'Open this door!'

No one took any notice. Sophie was looking at the window.

'Look! This window is rotten. I think we could get out!'

The window had been nailed shut. The girls were able to work out the nails. They pushed the window up and jumped through.

'We're out!' said Sophie. 'But we're still inside the fence!'

They remembered the notice on the fence.
DANGER OF DEATH.

NOT FOR THE PUBLIC TO KNOW

TOP SECRET

ZONE 13 FILES ONLY

THROUGH THE MIST

It was getting dark. Nearby, the big gate was closed and guarded.

The building was surrounded by trees. A track went away from the fence. They decided to go that way, even though it went further inside the deadly area.

The track soon came out of the trees into a wide clearing. Across the clearing it was misty.

They crossed the clearing. The mist was like a white wall. They didn't want to go into it. They remembered the notices on the fence.

'What's that?' said Sophie. They both listened.

It was the sound of a car, heading towards them!

'They've found out we've escaped! Quick, into the mist where they can't see us!'

The mist was very thick. They walked as quickly as they could.

The mist cleared. Suddenly, they were standing in blinding sunshine.

They stood still in amazement. When they had walked into the mist, it was getting dark. Now the sun was shining. They were in a

forest clearing. But they had never seen a forest like it.

It was very hot. They were soon sweating. There was a strange smell in the air. It was the smell of a swamp, full of rotting things.

The trees were nothing like the ones in the forest outside the fence. They had huge, rough trunks and great ferny leaves sticking out of the top. Underneath them, smaller fern-like plants grew. All around them they heard the buzz of insects.

'Where on Earth are we?' whispered Chris in a horrified voice.

There was a sudden, terrible screaming. It came from above them. They looked up and saw something they had never seen before.

But they knew what it was.

Chris felt very faint and shaky.

'It's just impossible!' she said.

NOT FOR THE PUBLIC TO KNOW

TOP SECRET

THE SWAMP

The creature hadn't spotted them. It floated in the hot air. Its huge leather wings seemed to glide rather than beat. Its long, pointed head was looking from side to side.

The girls had seen pictures of the creature. It was a pterosaur, a flying reptile from the time of the dinosaurs! They had been extinct for millions of years – but this one was definitely alive!

Suddenly, it saw them. It swept down. Its mouth was open, and they could see long, wicked-looking teeth.

'Quick, into the trees!'

They rushed into the shelter of the big tree ferns and crouched down. They could hear the pterosaur screaming. It didn't seem able to fly through the trees.

'Let's go a bit deeper.'

They pushed through the thick ferns.
Clouds of insects flew up. They bit the girls all
over.

Sophie was in the lead. She walked out
over an open piece of ground. Suddenly, she
was sinking into a stinking swamp!

'Help! I can't get out!'

Sophie was up to her waist in the swamp. She was slowly sinking.

Chris hung on to a strong fern and held out her hand. Sophie just managed to grab hold of it. Chris tugged and tugged. Her hands were muddy and slippery and it was difficult to hang on. Inch by inch, she pulled Sophie out of the mud.

At last, with a sucking sound she was out.

'Look at your legs!'

Sophie was wearing shorts. Her legs were covered with blood. Huge black leeches were stuck all over them, sucking her blood. She tried to pull them off, but they were fixed into her flesh.

Chris knew how to deal with them. She opened the pouch on her belt. Good! Matches! She lit a match. She held the flame next to the leeches. They dropped off straight away.

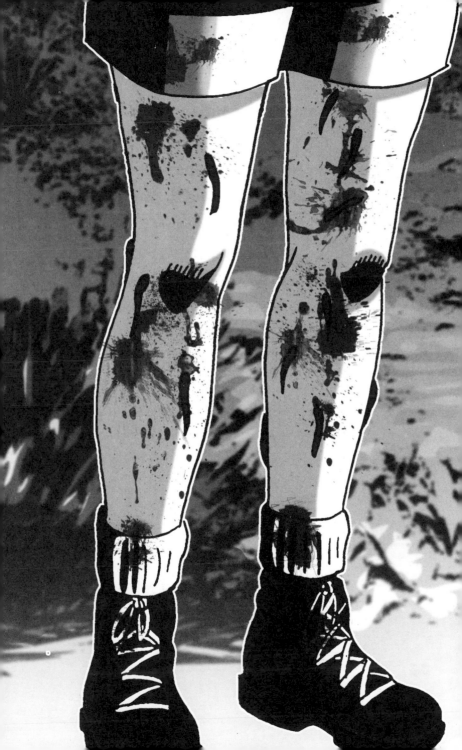

Sophie was trying to be brave. Her legs were very painful. The biting insects made it worse.

'We've got to get back,' she said.

They pushed their way back, the way they had come. The pterosaur seemed to have given up. In the distance, they could hear a great roaring and the thud of huge feet.

Then they heard a voice calling them.

THE EXPERIMENT THAT WENT WRONG

Even being locked up was better than this. The girls ran shouting towards the voice.

Someone was waiting for them. They couldn't tell who it was. He was wearing a white suit, with a square window over his face. The voice was muffled.

'Thank goodness you've come!' wailed Sophie.

'I'm sorry,' said the mystery person. 'I can't help you. I've just come to tell you why. I'm one of the soldiers. I'm not meant to be here.'

'Why can't you help us?' said Chris. 'What is this place? We've got to get out of here.'

'I don't know much about it,' said the soldier. 'It's a gateway into the past. It suddenly appeared in this forest. No one knows how it happened. I think it was an experiment that went wrong.

'We have to guard it. It's not the dinosaurs we're worried about. It's the germs and diseases. People today would have no resistance. Millions of people could die! That's why I have to wear this suit.'

'But what about us?'

'I've brought you food. But I can't let you come back. You've got to stay here. I've come to warn you. If you go back through the gateway, the boss will have you killed and your bodies will be burnt.'

He put down a package and turned to go.

'You can't leave us here to die!'

They couldn't see his face, but his voice sounded sorry. He walked to a place where the air seemed to shake. In a second, he had disappeared.

Chris picked up the package. She dropped it and screamed as a giant centipede scuttled away. Neither of them felt hungry, but they thought they had better eat. They might not get anything else. They sat on a rock and ate the sandwiches the soldier had brought.

In the distance, they could hear the thud of huge feet, and the crash of knocked-down trees. They looked at each other. The sound was getting closer.

They turned and ran. They were careful not to fall into another swamp. Luckily, the ground was rockier here, and there were fewer trees.

There was a terrible roaring behind them. Whatever it was, it was gaining on them! 'Look!'

Sophie had seen a dark hole in the side of the hill. They rushed towards it. It was their only chance.

THE CAVE

They rushed into the small cave. They stood in the darkness, listening. It knew they were in there! There was a roaring at the entrance, and the terrible smell of the creature's breath. Then they saw a huge eye in a scaly face.

The creature roared again. There was a crash as the great head hit the outside of the cave. The girls heard a rumbling sound, then more crashes.

The entrance to the cave was blocked with rock!

Both girls knew that this was the end.

Sophie wouldn't give up though. She asked Chris to light a match.

'Let's see where this cave goes.'

They walked away from the entrance. Chris felt the match burn her fingers. She dropped it and lit another one.

The cave split in two.

'Which way?'

The question was answered by a deep growling ahead of them. Something was living in the cave! They ran down another passage. They tripped and felt themselves falling. There was a splash. They were struggling in deep water!

'Chris, where are you?'

Sophie reached out and managed to grab Chris's arm.

'We've had it now! The matches are soaked!'

The strange thing was, it wasn't completely dark. They could make out a small hole at the side of the cave. A faint light was shining through it.

The girls hauled themselves out of the water. They could just squeeze through the hole. Some way ahead, they could see a flickering light.

They wriggled painfully along the tunnel. Water kept splashing over their faces. It was hard to breathe.

Sophie was in the lead.

She noticed something strange. The water in the tunnel was now flowing the other way – away from their faces! The tunnel seemed different now, too – the walls were quite smooth.

The light got brighter. They crawled out into daylight – and knew just where they were.

It was early morning. Birds were singing in the trees. A squirrel jumped from one branch to another. Behind them was the fence, with its warning notice. Water gushed out of the big pipe they had just crawled out of.

'It's another gateway! One they don't know about! We're free!'

The girls moved away from the fence, in case the soldiers came back. They found a hidden place, and lay down to rest in the morning sunshine.

'What was that soldier saying about germs and diseases?' Sophie asked.

'I don't know. Anyway, I feel fine.'

It was much later when they started to feel sick, and found a strange red rash spreading all over their bodies.

A month later, a million people were dying.

ABOUT THE AUTHOR

David Orme is an expert on strange, unexplained events. For his protection (and yours) we cannot show a photograph of him.

David created the Zone 13 files to record the cases he studied. Some of these files really do involve aliens, but many do not. Aliens are not everywhere. Just in most places.

These stories are all taken from the Zone 13 files. They will not be here for long. Read them while you can.

But don't close your eyes when you go to sleep at night. **They** will be watching you.